D0604419

GERSHON'S MONSTER

— A Story for the Jewish New Year —

Retold by ERIC A. KIMMEL • Illustrated by JON J MUTH

SCHOLASTIC PRESS   NEW YORK

With deepest gratitude we acknowledge the following people:
Debbie Friedman for her insightful suggestions; Rabbi Benay Lappe
for her concise and accessible "Six Steps for Doing T'Shuvah," adapted
from Chapter Two of Rambam's Laws of Repentance; and Rabbi
Roderick Young from Congregation Beth Simchat Torah
for reviewing the text in its final form.

The illustrator gratefully acknowledges Julianna, Nikolai, and Adelaine
for posing, Bonnie for her inspiration, and Daniel Hartz for his courage.

LIBRARY OF CONGRESS CATALOGING-IN-PUBLICATION DATA
Kimmel, Eric A.
Gershon's monster: a story for the Jewish New Year / retold by Eric A. Kimmel;
illustrated by Jon J Muth.   p. cm.
Retelling of a Hasidic legend featuring Rabbi Israel ben Eliezer—Author's note.
Summary: When his sins threaten the lives of his beloved twin children,
a Jewish man finally repents of his wicked ways.
ISBN 0-439-10839-X
[1. Jews—Folklore. 2. Folklore.] I. Muth, Jon J, ill.
II. Ba'al Shem Tov, ca. 1700–1760. III. Title.
PZ8.1.K567 Mo 2000
398.2'089'924
99-046986

10 9 8 7 6 5 4 3 2 1   0/0 01 02 03
Printed in Mexico 49 · First edition, September 2000

An earlier version of this story was published in *Cricket* magazine.
The text was set in 14-point Truesdell Bold and the display type was set in Blackfriar.
The illustrations in this book were rendered in watercolor.
Book design by David Saylor

To Rosemary and Yair Alroy — E. A. K.

For Allen Spiegel — J. J. M.

The city of Constantsa stands on the shores of the Black Sea.
Many years ago, a man named Gershon and his wife, Fayga, lived there.

Now Gershon was not always the best person he could be. True, the
mistakes he made were not huge. They were common, ordinary things: a
broken promise, a temper lost for no reason, a little untruth told here and
there.

But unlike most people, Gershon never regretted what he did. He never
apologized or asked anyone's forgiveness.

This way of behaving became a habit. Gershon paid no attention to how he treated others and he didn't care. For he could shed his mistakes and thoughtless acts like a dog sheds hair. Every Friday, Gershon swept them up and tossed them into the cellar.

Then, once a year on Rosh Hashanah, he stuffed them into a sack, dragged the enormous bundle down to the sea, and tossed it in.

But selfishness and thoughtless deeds are never disposed of so easily. There is always a price to pay, as Gershon was about to learn.

Now Gershon was a baker, an important man in town. But he and his wife were childless. They wanted a child more than anything in the world.

One day, Gershon's wife heard of a *tzaddik*, a wonder rabbi, who lived in the town of Kuty. "Perhaps the *tzaddik* can give us a child," Fayga said to her husband.

"I will go to Kuty and see," Gershon answered.

Gershon harnessed his horse to the wagon and set out.

The journey took many days. Gershon asked a stranger how to get to the *tzaddik*'s house. Of course, he didn't say, "Thank you."

When Gershon arrived, he barged through the door without knocking. The *tzaddik* was in his study. "My wife and I want a child," said Gershon. "I hear you can help us. Name your price. I'll pay."

The *tzaddik* frowned and said, "One does not buy children the way one buys chickens. But your wife is a good woman. For her sake, I will see if anything can be done."

The *tzaddik* closed his eyes and began to pray. Gershon fidgeted impatiently. The clock on the wall ticked away the minutes.

At last, the *tzaddik* opened his eyes.

"Be thankful for all that you have. Do not ask for more."

"What kind of answer is that?" Gershon cried. "If God cannot give me a child, at least tell me the reason why!"

The *tzaddik*'s eyes searched the depths of Gershon's soul. "Did you think you could live so thoughtlessly forever? The sea cries out because you have polluted her waters! God is angry with you. Accept God's judgment. Your recklessness will bring your children more sorrow than you can imagine."

"I will take that risk," Gershon said selfishly.

"Foolish man. I will do what you ask, but you will regret it."

The *tzaddik* took a piece of parchment and wrote upon it with a quill pen. After the ink dried, he folded the parchment in half and gave it to Gershon. "Have your wife wear this around her neck. In one year's time she will give birth to twins, a boy and a girl. They will be all you desire. They will be with you for five years."

"And then?" Gershon asked. "What strange prophecy is this? If something is going to harm my children, tell me now so I can protect them."

"You cannot protect them," the *tzaddik* said. "On the morning of their fifth birthday, they will go down to the sea. . . ." He paused. "Enjoy your precious children while you can. Do not ask for more."

Gershon threw himself at the *tzaddik*'s feet. "What will happen at the sea?" Gershon pleaded. "At least give me a sign!"

The *tzaddik* spoke with a steady voice. "The day you put two stockings on one foot and storm around the house looking for the missing stocking is the day your children will . . . enough! I can say no more!"

Gershon kissed the *tzaddik*'s hand. "Holy man, you have saved my children's lives. I will remember your words and be watchful. Furthermore, I will repent for all my wrongdoings."

The *tzaddik* shook his head. "You will forget everything as soon as you return home. Go now, unhappy man. I can do nothing for you."

Gershon returned home. Just as the *tzaddik* predicted, he soon forgot
everything except the promise of children. Fayga wore the charm faithfully. In a
year's time she gave birth to twins. They were the most beautiful children
Gershon and his wife had ever seen. They named the boy Joseph and the girl
Sarah. The twins grew up healthy and strong. They spent whole summers at
the beach, running on the sand and swimming in the sparkling water.

And Gershon went on behaving as recklessly as ever, sweeping his thoughtless acts into the cellar. And once a year, on Rosh Hashanah, he stuffed them into a sack and dragged them down to the sea.

Five years passed. One August morning, Gershon awoke with the sun pouring in his window. It was scarcely eight o'clock, yet the air hung heavy with heat. Gershon reached for his clothes. He pulled on his shirt, then his trousers, and finally his left stocking. The heat made his head swim. He sat down on the bed to collect himself, and without thinking, took his right stocking and drew it over his left foot. Then he started to put on his shoes. "Where is my other stocking?" Gershon grumbled when he noticed that his right foot was bare. "Who has taken it?" he roared as he stormed through the house.

Fayga laughed. "No one has taken your stocking. Look at your feet. You have put two stockings on one foot."

Gershon's face suddenly turned pale as he remembered the *tzaddik*'s prophecy. "Where are the children?" he cried frantically.

"At the seashore, where they always are."

As soon as Gershon heard the words "at the seashore," he ran out the door.

"Come back!" Fayga cried. "You forgot your shoes!"

But Gershon had no time for shoes. He tore down the path to the beach.

"Dear God," he cried, "let me not be too late."

And then he saw them, Sarah and Joseph, playing at the water's edge.
Gershon cupped his hands to his mouth and shouted, "Come away from there!"
But he was out of breath, and his voice did not carry far. The children waved
and went back to their play. Sarah chased Joseph into the water.

All at once, the sky grew dark, as if a cloud had covered the sun. But it was no cloud. Gershon saw it rising from the sea: an immense black monster covered with scales like iron plates. On each scale was written one of Gershon's misdeeds. "Father! Save us!" the children cried out as the monster came toward them.

Gershon ran as he had never run before. He pushed the children aside and threw himself down before the monster. Looking up into the creature's glittering eyes, he pleaded for forgiveness.

"I know what you are. You are my pride and selfishness coming back to me, just as the *tzaddik* foretold. Please have mercy. Spare my children. Why punish them for my thoughtless deeds? Take me instead."

For the first time in his life, Gershon truly felt sorry for all of his
wrongdoings. Heartbroken, he kneeled before the monster and awaited his end.
But it never came. The monster rose into the air like a great cloud. Its scales
melted into raindrops that fell like a summer shower, cleansing the sea.

Gershon carried Sarah and Joseph home to breakfast. The whole family blessed their food and offered thanks for God's mercy.

Then Gershon went down into his cellar and scrubbed each crack and corner until every trace of his old ways was gone. He scrubbed his soul, too, until it shined like a pair of Sabbath candlesticks. Never again did he throw another bundle into the sea. And never again did he see the monster.

When Joseph and Sarah grew up, they made sure to tell this story to their children every Rosh Hashanah, as I am now telling it to you. Remember it. For if you keep your soul clean, your best self will always shine through as surely as raindrops cleanse the sea.

Author's Note

This story is a retelling of one of the earliest Hasidic legends. The "wonder rabbi" whom Gershon visits is based on Rabbi Israel ben Eliezer (c.1700–1760), the founder of the Hasidic movement in Judaism. He is also known as the Ba'al Shem Tov, meaning "Master of the Good Name." My ancestors lived in the same region in Poland where he began his mission. They undoubtedly knew of him.

The idea of casting one's sins into the sea (as Gershon does in the story) is derived from an old Jewish ceremony called *tashlikh*. On the afternoon of the first day of Rosh Hashanah, the beginning of the Jewish New Year, people gather by lakes or rivers or at the seashore to recite biblical verses concerning repentance and forgiveness. Some turn their pockets inside out, allowing bread crumbs inside to fall into the water to be eaten by fishes. This symbolizes the casting off of sins.

However, our misdeeds cannot be forgiven unless we are truly sorry and make every effort to right whatever wrong has been done. This is called *t'shuvah*.

T'shuvah is usually translated as "repentance." The word actually means "to return." When we fall short of being our best selves, we are haunted by our conscience, as Gershon is symbolically haunted by the monster in the story. Going through the process of *t'shuvah* permits us to erase our mistakes and "return" to our true moral nature. These are the steps we must follow:

1. Admit that we have done wrong.
2. Feel remorse.
3. Resolve in our hearts never to act this way again.
4. Make every effort to right the wrong we have done.
5. Apologize and ask forgiveness from those we have wronged.
6. Make every effort to relieve whatever pain or distress we might have caused others.

When we can confront the same situation, but this time do what is right, we have completed the process of *t'shuvah*. We have returned to our best selves.